The books in this series introduce young children to the four rules of number.

This book gives over one hundred basic facts of subtraction. The lively, colourful cartoon pictures illustrate the number bonds and mathematical symbols are used under each picture. There are hours of fun and learning for all young children who love counting and simple arithmetic.

First edition

Ladybird Junior Maths
SUBTRACTION

written by
ROGER and MARY HURT
illustrated by
PETER KINGSTON

6 − 5

Ladybird Books Loughborough

Here are two elephants.

If one elephant
runs away,

there will be one elephant left.

$$2 - 1 = 1$$

Here are three children.

When the little boy goes home,
there will be two children left.

$$3 - 1 = 2$$

Daddy has one egg
and he drops it
on the floor.

Now he has
no eggs
in his hand.

$$1 - 1 = 0$$

There are four cats.

If one cat runs away,
there will be three cats left.

$$4 - 1 = 3$$

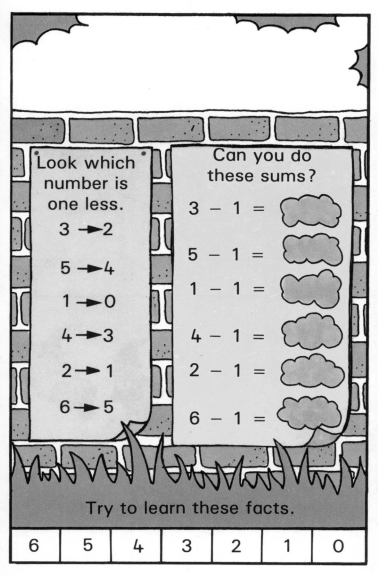

Look which number is one less.

3 ➔ 2

5 ➔ 4

1 ➔ 0

4 ➔ 3

2 ➔ 1

6 ➔ 5

Can you do these sums?

3 − 1 =

5 − 1 =

1 − 1 =

4 − 1 =

2 − 1 =

6 − 1 =

Try to learn these facts.

| 6 | 5 | 4 | 3 | 2 | 1 | 0 |

I have two sweets.

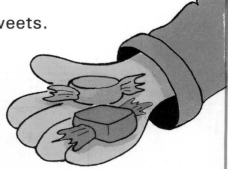

I don't eat either of them
so I still have two sweets.

$$2 - 0 = 2$$

Here are four witches.

If two witches fly away,
there will be two witches left.

$$4 - 2 = 2$$

There are three birds on a branch and they fly away.

Now there are no birds on the branch.

$$3 - 3 = 0$$

There are two bottles on the step.

If Mummy takes them inside,
there will be no bottles on the step.

$$2 - 2 = 0$$

There are five shirts on the line.

If two shirts blow away,
there will be three shirts on the line.

$$5 - 2 = 3$$

Here are five dragons.

When three dragons run away,
there are two dragons left.

$$5 - 3 = 2$$

Here are five ice-creams.

Four ice-creams
will soon be eaten.
There is one ice-cream left.

$$5 - 4 = 1$$

There are five mice.
If a cat chases them away,

there will be no mice.

$$5 - 5 = 0$$

Which fish are caught in the nets?

13

A farmer has six lambs.

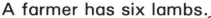

If he sends
three lambs to market,
he will have three lambs left.

$$6 - 3 = 3$$

We have six lollipops.

If the children eat two lollipops,
there will be four lollipops left.

$$6 - 2 = 4$$

There are six logs.

When one log is taken away,
there are five logs left.

$$6 - 1 = 5$$

There are six rabbits in the field.

No rabbits run away.
There are still six rabbits.

$$6 - 0 = 6$$

6 − 0 = 6

Take away from six.

6 − 2 = 4

6 − 3 = 3

6 − 5 = 1

6 − 4 = 2

6 − 6 = 0

6 − 1 = 5

Try to remember these.

There were seven leaves on a branch.

Three leaves blew away.
Now there are four leaves
on the branch.

$$7 - 3 = 4$$

A clown had seven balloons.

Four balloons burst.
Now he has three balloons.

$$7 - 4 = 3$$

There were seven ladybirds on a leaf.

Two ladybirds flew away.
Now there are five ladybirds
on the leaf.

$$7 - 2 = 5$$

Here are the seven dwarfs.
Five dwarfs are going to work.

There are two dwarfs
left at home.

$$7 - 5 = 2$$

Count back two.

5 → 3

8 → 6

3 → 1

9 → 7

10 → 8

7 → 5

2 → 0

6 → 4

4 → 2

Can you do these sums?

5 − 2 =

6 − 2 =

8 − 2 =

3 − 2 =

10 − 2 =

9 − 2 =

4 − 2 =

7 − 2 =

2 − 2 =

| 10 | 9 | 8 | 7 | 6 | 5 | 4 | 3 | 2 | 1 | 0 |

20

There were eight balls on the shelf.

Three balls rolled away.
Now there are five balls.

$$8 - 3 = 5$$

There were eight books on the shelf.

Sam took one book away.
Now there are seven books on the shelf.

$$8 - 1 = 7$$

Take away from eight.

8−8=0

8−6=2

8−4=4

8−0=8

8−2=6

8−1=7

8−5=3

8−3=5

8−7=1

Try to remember these.

Here are nine bananas.
A monkey takes six.

There are three
bananas left.

$$9 - 6 = 3$$

Here are nine bees.

When eight fly away
there is one bee at the honey pot.

$$9 - 8 = 1$$

8 – 0

9 – 1

8 – 2

9 – 3

9 – 2

8 – 1

7

6

8

Which clowns are holding the balloons?

8 − 4

9 − 7

9 − 4

8 − 3

8 − 6

9 − 5

2   4   5

Take away from nine.

Try to remember these.

What are the missing numbers?

9 − ☁ = 3

8 − ☁ = 4

7 − ☁ = 2

9 − ☁ = 4

8 − ☁ = 6

7 − ☁ = 4

9 − ☁ = 8

8 − ☁ = 8

7 − ☁ = 0

9
8
7
6
5
4
3
2
1

0

Daniel has ten crayons.
He gives Kate
four crayons.

Now he has
six crayons.

10 − 4 = 6

Kate has ten crayons.
She gives Daniel
six crayons.

Now she has
four crayons.

10 − 6 = 4

Daniel has ten crayons.
He gives seven
crayons to Kate.

10 CRAYONS

Now he has
three crayons.

$$10 - 7 = 3$$

Kate has ten crayons.
She gives three
crayons to Daniel.

10 CRAYONS

Now she has
seven crayons.

$$10 - 3 = 7$$

Daniel has ten crayons. He gives Kate nine crayons.

Now he has one crayon.

10 CRAYONS

$$10 - 9 = 1$$

Kate has ten crayons. She gives one crayon to Daniel.

Now she has nine crayons.

10 CRAYONS

$$10 - 1 = 9$$

Daniel has ten crayons.
He gives Kate
eight crayons.

Now he has
two crayons.

10 − 8 = 2

Kate has ten crayons.
She gives Daniel
two crayons.

Now she has
eight crayons.

10 − 2 = 8

31

Some trees have been chopped down.

11 − 9 = 2   11 − 2 = 9

11 − 7 = 4   11 − 4 = 7

12 − 7 = 5   12 − 5 = 7

12 − 9 = 3   12 − 3 = 9

The leaves are falling from the branches.

$11 - 6 = 5$

$11 - 5 = 6$

$11 - 8 = 3$

$11 - 3 = 8$

12 − 8 = 4   12 − 4 = 8

12 − 10 = 2   12 − 2 = 10

Who lives in the houses?

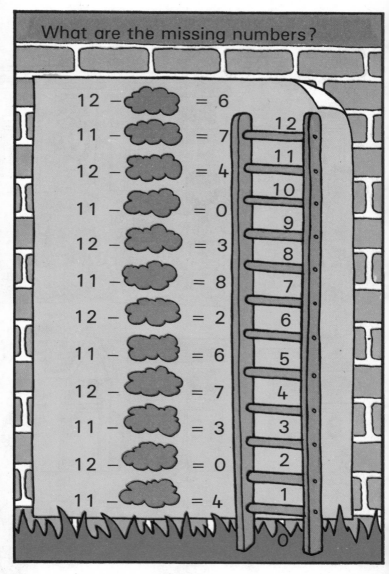

40

There are some buttons missing.

13 − 9 = 4   13 − 4 = 9   13 − 8 = 5

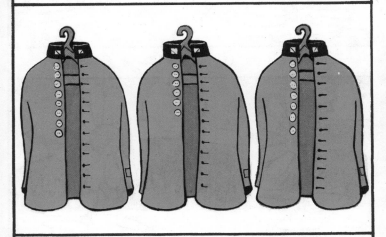

13 − 5 = 8   13 − 7 = 6   13 − 6 = 7

14 − 9 = 5   14 − 5 = 9

14 − 8 = 6   14 − 6 = 8

14 − 7 = 7   14 − 4 = 10

42

What are the missing numbers?

14 − ___ = 5

13 − 5 = ___

13 − ___ = 4

___ − 6 = 8

13 − ___ = 6

14 − 8 = ___

___ − 6 = 7

14 − 5 = ___

13 − ___ = 5

14 − 7 = ___

13 − ___ = 7

___ − 4 = 10

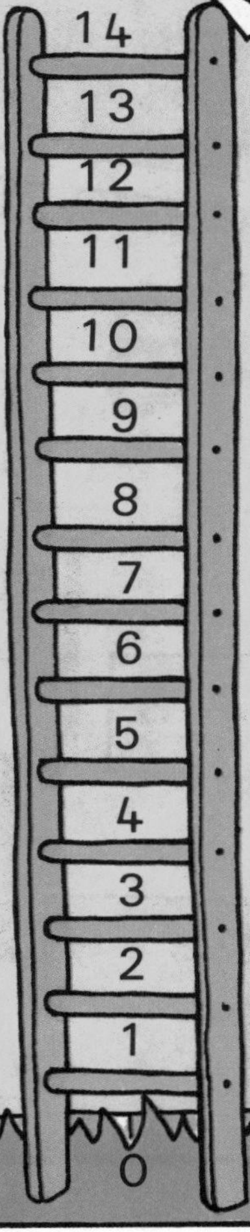
14
13
12
11
10
9
8
7
6
5
4
3
2
1
0

Which flags go on which sand castles

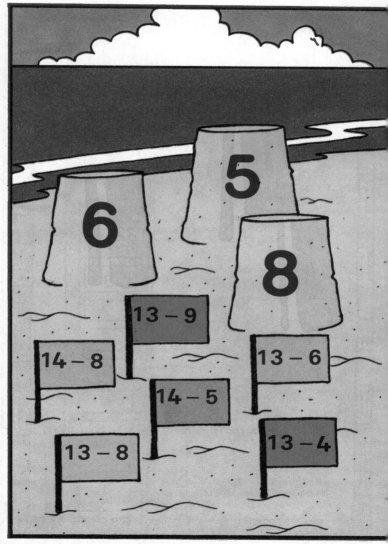

45

Count the unbroken window panes.

15 − 9 = 6

16 − 9 = 7

16 − 8 = 8

15 − 7 = 8

15 − 6 = 9

16 − 6 = 10   16 − 7 = 9

15 − 8 = 7

Paints
18 − 10 = 8

Crayons
18 − 9 = 9

48

Coats
17 − 8 = 9

Children
17 − 9 = 8

Can you put the books away?

51